D1491444

Kansas City, MO Public Library

0000180311272

Exploring Materials

Rock

Abby Colich

Heinemann
LIBRARY
Chicago, Illinois

© 2014 Heinemann Library
an imprint of Capstone Global Library, LLC
Chicago, Illinois

To contact Capstone Global Library please phone 800-747-4992, or
visit our website www.capstonepub.com

All rights reserved. No part of this publication may be reproduced or
transmitted in any form or by any means, electronic or mechanical,
including photocopying, recording, taping, or any information
storage and retrieval system, without permission in writing from the
publisher.

Edited by Abby Colich, Daniel Nunn, and Catherine Veitch
Designed by Marcus Bell
Picture research by Tracy Cummins
Production by Victoria Fitzgerald
Originated by Capstone Global Library Ltd
Printed in the United States of America in North Mankato, Minnesota
042014   008147RP

Library of Congress Cataloging-in-Publication Data
Colich, Abby.
  Rock / Abby Colich.
    pages cm.—(Exploring materials)
  Includes bibliographical references and index.
  ISBN 978-1-4329-8018-4 (hb)—ISBN 978-1-4329-8026-9 (pb) 1.
Rocks—Juvenile literature. I. Title.

  QE432.2.C64 2014
  620.1′32—dc23   2012047493

Acknowledgments
The author and publisher are grateful to the following for permission
to reproduce copyright material: Shutterstock pp. 4 (© orxy), 5
(© ross-edward cairney), 6 (© ermess), 7a (© Ho Yeow Hui), 7b
(© Bejim), 7c (© Natalia Bratslavsky), 7d (© Brian K.), 8 (© Matyas
Arvai), 9 (© Dumitrescu Ciprian-Florin), 10 (© Goluba), 11 (©
IMAGENFX), 12 (© Golden Pixels LLC), 13 (© Juha-Pekka Kervinen),
14 (© RUI FERREIRA), 15 (© Andreja Donko), 16 (© Patryk Kosmider),
17 (© feiyuwzhangjie), 18 (© Marie C Fields), 19r (© Ruslan Kudrin),
19l (© Chianuri), 20 (Ariy), 21 (© Coffeemill), 22 (© Ivica Drusany, ©
Evgeniya Uvarova, © Shaun Dodds), 23a (© Andreja Donko), 23b (©
Marie C Fields).

Cover photograph of a boy stacking a pile of stones reproduced
with permission of Getty Images (© Geoff Brighting). Back cover
photograph reproduced with permission of Shutterstock (© Marie C
Fields).

We would like to thank Valarie Akerson, Nancy Harris, Dee Reid,
and Diana Bentley for their invaluable help in the preparation of
this book.

Every effort has been made to contact copyright holders of any
material reproduced in this book. Any omissions will be rectified in
subsequent printings if notice is given to the publisher.

Contents

What Is Rock?

Rock is a material.

Materials are what things are made from.

There are many different kinds of rock.

Rock can be made into many
different things.

Where Does Rock Come From?

Rock is found in nature.

Rock is found underground.

Rock is found underwater.

People dig rock out of the ground.

What Is Rock Like?

chalk

Rock can be soft or hard.
Chalk is soft rock.

smooth

Rock can be smooth or rough.

Rock can break into smaller pieces.

Rock can be carved into
different shapes.

How Do We Use Rock?

We use rock to build houses.

We use rock to build bridges.

Chalk comes from rock.

rock salt

table salt

Some salt comes from rock.

We use rock to make art.

We use rock to make jewelry.

Quiz

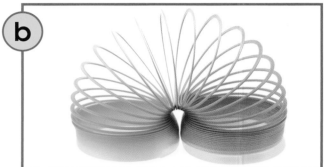

Which of these things are made from rock?

Answer on page 24.

Picture Glossary

carve cut into shapes

chalk soft rock. Chalk can be used for drawing.

Index

The **chalk (a)** and **stones (c)** are made from rock.

Notes for Parents and Teachers
Before reading
Ask children if they have heard the term "material" and what they think it means. Reinforce the concept of materials. Explain that all objects are made from different materials. A material is something that takes up space and can be used to make other things. Ask children to give examples of different materials. These may include metal, wood, and rock.

To get children interested in the topic, ask if they know what rock is. Identify any misconceptions they may have. Ask them to think about whether their ideas might change as the book is read.

After reading
- Check to see if any of the identified misconceptions have changed.
- Show the children examples of rock, including chalk, salt, and pebbles.
- Pass the different objects around. Ask the children to describe the properties of each object. What color is the rock? Is it heavy or light? Big or small? Discuss other words for rock such as stone and pebble.